Just My Luck

Holiday Romance, Volume 4

Brill Harper

Published by Brill Harper, 2024.

This is a work of fiction. Similarities to real people, places, or events are entirely coincidental.

JUST MY LUCK

First edition. February 29, 2024.

Copyright © 2024 Brill Harper.

ISBN: 979-8224464296

Written by Brill Harper.

About this Book

———

I'M NOT SURE IF THIS little green dress is a lucky charm or a curse. The scrap of fabric is the catalyst of the most humiliating St. Patrick's Day of my life (curse). In which I had to be rescued by my best friend's older brother (curse). Whom I've had a crush on since I was ten (curse, also, but can hardly blame the dress).

But he's looking at me a lot differently than he did when I hid all my curves under baggy clothes (lucky). And now we're stranded in his house during an ice storm (lucky). And I think I might finally lose my V status (lucky).

But he also has a VERY BIG PROBLEM (curse) that makes him a locker room joke of envious men, a novelty item for only the bravest of women, and not a very good starter model for a girl with untried womanhood (curse curse curse).

But rearranging a few internal organs to make room for love is a small price to pay, right?

Author Confession: Best friend's older brother, forced proximity, and BDE are a few of my favorite things. Sometimes, when two people are meant to be together, true love requires them to work together to make all the pieces fit.

One

Ginger

ST. PATRICK'S DAY

There is no way in hell I can wear this dress.

It's super sexy, and I can't pull off super sexy. I can't even pull off *almost* sexy. Super sexy is a bridge too far.

"Oh my God, GinGin. You need to wear that tonight. That color of green is fire on you," says my best friend, Jules, as she twirls around in her own mini-dress.

I roll my eyes. "You have said that about every dress I tried on."

I still think jeans and a hoodie would be fine. But that is why Jules won't let me dress myself and has made me try on a bajillion dresses from her closet.

"That's because it's true. You look great in all of them. But trust me, Ginger, you'll turn heads in that dress."

I take a deep breath and look at myself in the mirror. The dress hugs every curve of my body and the deep V-neckline plunges down to nearly my belly button. I feel exposed and vulnerable, but at the same time, there's a thrill that runs through me at the thought of wearing something so daring.

Jules sees the hesitation on my face and walks over to me. "Come on, GinGin. It's time to step out of your comfort zone. You deserve to feel sexy and confident."

I nod slowly, still unsure if I can pull it off.

"Are you sure I don't look too slutty?"

"You look just the right amount of slutty," she says. "Also, are you saying my clothes are slutty?"

One side-eye is all she needs to burst out laughing. Jules is not exactly a classy girl. Which suits her just fine. She has no problem flaunting her assets and using her looks to get what she wants. But that's not me. I've always been the quiet one, the bookish one. And, truth be told, I've always been a little envious of Jules's confidence.

But tonight, in this dress, I feel like I could be someone else entirely. Someone bold and daring, someone who isn't afraid to take risks. Maybe I will even create that Ignitr account Jules has been bugging me to try.

Probably not. I don't think I'm ready for hook-up culture.

Ideally, I want someone a few years older than me. Someone who thinks brains are as sexy as tits. Someone who will be exclusive and who wants to teach me everything I've been missing out on. This special someone is also going to have to be able to take me out of my head so all this can happen. And that is no easy task. I'll need shock and awe for sure. Because this nerdy girl is very trapped in her head.

That's a lot to put on a dating app profile.

Jules claps her hands together. "Let's finish the look." She pulls out a pair of stiletto heels from her closet and hands them to me. "These will elongate your legs and make you look like a goddess."

"And break my neck, but sure, why not."

I slip them on and stand up straighter, feeling the power of the heels and the dress combined. I stare at myself in the mirror, feeling like a completely different person. The reflection staring back at me is a far cry from my usual reserved self.

Jules grins. "See? I told you. You look amazing."

I can feel my cheeks heating up with a blush. "Thanks, Jules. I don't know if I can handle the attention though."

"Don't worry. I'll be there to take at least half the attention away from you." She pumps up her boobs in her dress. "You're going to get that V-card punched for sure tonight. It's your lucky night and that is your lucky dress."

My virginity is something that I've held onto for a long time. It's not that I haven't had opportunities, but I've always been too scared to take that step. Jules, on the other hand, has had her fair share of experiences and always encourages me to take a chance.

Now, as I near my twentieth birthday, virginity seems like a brick weighing me down. The longer I don't have sex, the more nervous about having sex I am. And the more nervous about having sex I am, the longer I put off having it.

"Let's do makeup and pre-funk," she suggests.

I nod, following her to the bathroom where she starts applying makeup to my face after I put in my dreaded contact lenses. I hate wearing them so much. I close my eyes and let her work her magic. As she finishes up, I catch a glimpse of myself in the mirror and can hardly believe the transformation. I look like a completely different person, sultry and alluring.

I skip the offered drink, though. I'm not used to wearing heels and it's spitting ice outside. I don't want to spend the holiday in the emergency room.

The party we decided on is at one of the pubs in the next town over because we live in a college town and we're frankly tired of college guys. They are immature and mostly frat bros. Jules is tired of frat bros. I am tired of frat bros.

And frat bros have zero interest in the quiet awkward girl in the front row of class anyway.

When we arrive, the Uber drops us off across the street. The pub is already packed, with people spilling out onto the sidewalk. Jules takes my hand and pulls me towards the crosswalk.

"Remember, tonight is all about having fun and letting loose. Don't worry about anything else," she whispers in my ear.

I nod, trying to calm the butterflies in my stomach.

"Shit. I left my purse in the car. Go ahead. I'm right behind you," I tell her.

I turn back and gesture for the driver to roll down the window and lean into the car to explain. He reaches behind him and grabs my purse. I'm so grateful he hadn't already gone. Getting stranded outside this bar with no ID (fake), no money (not a lot anyway, but none would be worse), and no way to get home is not the kind of lucky I'm hoping to get tonight.

I walk back to the crosswalk but hit a sudden onslaught of nerves while I wait for the light to change. I take a deep breath and remind myself that I can do this. I don't have to be nerdy and shy all the time. I can be a lucky goddess.

Do lucky goddesses get arrested for prostitution while crossing the street?

Asking for a friend.

Two

Duncan

LATER THAT NIGHT

Ginger is shivering in the truck seat next to me. She should have thought of that before she put on that fucking dress. What was she thinking?

"What were you thinking?" I ask, throwing the truck into drive.

"It was just a party, Duncan," she explains.

"You're lucky you got arrested for prostitution before you made it into the bar. You wouldn't have gotten out of the underage drinking charges if you'd been arrested inside the bar."

"Yes, lucky. That's exactly how I'm feeling. How fortunate that I was arrested for prostitution this evening. What a stroke of luck."

I ignore her sarcasm. "And you're damn lucky I was catching up on paperwork at the station tonight and could get the charges dropped."

I don't want to think of her in the tank. Luckily, my little sister's best friend didn't make it that far. I was able to fix things for her as soon as I heard what was happening, and she was released into my care without being formally booked.

She hides her face in her hands. "Are you going to tell my parents?"

That's when I realize she's crying. Damn it. I don't have any defense for crying girls. Woman, I guess. She didn't look like a girl when I saw her in that dress.

Fuck. I've seen bathing suits with more coverage.

It made me feel so dirty to even look at her like that. But I couldn't help it. She's grown up so much since the last time I saw her. No more braces. No more glasses. No more teen acne. Her long hair falls in soft waves down her back instead of the frizzy mess she used to keep in pigtails most of the time. And her figure...wow. Her curves are in all the right places. I try not to think about it, but how can I not? She's practically begging for attention in a dress like that.

I have no doubt that the dress, if you can call it that, is borrowed from my sister Jules' closet. Ginger has always been a good girl. I've never worried about her being a bad influence on my sister...it's always been the other way around. I've always been grateful that someone with common sense has my crazy sister's back.

Usually has common sense.

I'm guessing Jules talked her into this. Jules is probably still at the damn bar, even. But Ginger won't give her up, and I don't especially want to bust my sister six months before she's twenty-one, so I'm not going to interrogate Ginger for an answer since I don't want to know.

"Ginger," I say, trying to keep my voice even. "Please don't cry."

She just shakes her head and snuffles on her tears. I root around the center console for a napkin from a fast food place and hand one to her.

"I'm not going to tell your parents. I should, but I won't. You didn't break the law. You were just..." She was just being fucking stupid. "The officer thought you were asking the Uber driver if he wanted a date. The way you were hanging inside his car window. The way you were dressed. That neighborhood has a lot of hookers. You fit right in."

She starts sobbing.

Fuck. Maybe that wasn't the nicest way to say it.

That dress, though. How does she keep her tits inside it? It's cut so low. All a guy has to do is push the fabric over an inch and out come the tits. And no way can she bend over without showing her pussy to the world.

My asshole dick pushes against my zipper thinking about her exposed like that. I never had that trouble with her before. Not when she wore her baggy shirts and too big glasses. Not when she was that awkward teenager who used to hang around Jules and got quiet whenever my friends and I were around.

I don't want her to be like this. I want her to be the same goofy but cute girl I knew. Not this smokeshow.

But now it's like I can't help thinking about her as a woman. A hot one. All I want to do is push that dress up and lick her right up the middle.

Stop it. I take a deep breath and concentrate really hard on not thinking about Ginger like that.

"Ginger," I say, my voice gruff. "You're going to have to be more careful. You can't just go around acting like a slut. You're better than that."

That turns her head. She looks at me, obviously pissed off. "A slut? You mean a woman who enjoys sex? Is that supposed to be disparaging? Is a man who enjoys sex a slut, too?"

I can't help but laugh at her indignation. Which of course pisses her off more.

"No," I say. "I just mean you shouldn't be so careless. People are going to make assumptions about you, and you have to be smart about how you present yourself."

She crosses her arms and looks away, obviously still mad. I sigh. I can't believe I'm even having this conversation with *Ginger*. Ginger the good one. Ginger the smart one. Ginger who's been hiding excellent tits under her hoodies.

"Look," I say, gentling my voice. "I'm sorry. I didn't mean to come across as judgmental. I realize I sound like an asshole from the last century. I just want you to be safe, okay?"

She turns her shoulders toward the window, no longer just content to look away from me with her eyes. She wants to ignore me with her whole body now.

I wish my body could fucking ignore her as easily.

"GinGin..."

"It wasn't as judgmental as it was misogynistic."

"You're right. I'm sorry. It scared me to think about what could have happened to you, but I shouldn't have tried to slut shame you. I'm not proud of it." I know better, too. My mom would wash my mouth out with soap for saying such a thing. My parents raised my sister and I with feminist values, and it sucks that my first gut reaction to fear was patriarchal bullshit.

"Do you forgive me?"

"Yes." But she still isn't looking at me.

I should just take her back to her dorm, but she's kind of in bad shape. I promised Jules I would take care of her, and I overheard Ginger on the phone making Jules promise she would stay out and have a good time without her. That she was fine. But she's not fine. And the roads are shit.

Fuck me. Why. Why couldn't I be a stock broker or something? Something far, far away from my troublesome sister and her usually mild-mannered best friend. Some kind of job where I wouldn't feel responsible for her.

Why couldn't she be going to school at some far-off Ivy League campus instead of the state school less than an hour away from our hometown? I guess I didn't get too far from home either. Right smack dab in the middle of our college alma mater and my folks' house.

She shivers.

"Are you cold?"

She shakes her head. I covered her in a sweatshirt I keep in my locker at the station when I was fixing her situation, but her feet must be ice cubes. The weather is typical for March, sunny and mild one day, winter storm the next. It's raining ice and the wind has picked up.

I don't like thinking about Jules and all the other green beer drunks getting home on roads that are quickly becoming ice rinks.

"Are you sure Jules is in a safe place? The roads are getting rough."

Ginger sighs heavily. "She's back on campus."

"In your dorm?"

"Not exactly."

She's hooking up. Shit. "Why travel all the way to town if you're just going to hook up with someone who lives on campus?"

Ginger shrugs.

A car in front of us spins out but luckily rights itself.

I let out a frustrated sigh and glance at Ginger. She looks up at me with big brown eyes, still red from crying. I can't be mad at her. She's just a kid.

No, not anymore she's not.

But she's also my sister's best friend, and I promised to take care of her tonight. My sister would expect it. My folks would expect it too.

There's no hope for it. I'm just going to have to bring the little prostitute home with me.

Three

———

Ginger

WHEN I HAVE PULLED myself together enough to look where we are going, I'm surprised I don't know the neighborhood.

"Where are we?" I ask Duncan.

Duncan the cop. Duncan my biggest crush since I was ten. Duncan who probably hates me now.

"My house."

"Your house? Why?"

"Because you're in no shape to go back to your dorm alone right now. I promised Jules I would take care of you, and I intend to keep that promise." Duncan's voice is firm, leaving no room for argument.

I nod, feeling grateful and embarrassed at the same time. "I didn't drink anything. I promise."

He doesn't say anything as we pull up to the curb.

"Just stay there until I help you out. The sidewalk is icy and your fucking shoes are ridiculous."

Mortifying. This whole night has been mortifying. I watch him as he rounds the front of the truck. Why does he have to be so attractive?

Duncan is the kind of man who exudes confidence and authority. He's tall and broad-shouldered, with a chiseled jawline and deep blue eyes. He's the kind of guy who could make any girl weak at the knees. I've seen his girlfriends over the years, and they are all so pretty. Usually blonde. Unfailingly extroverted.

And here I am, a sobbing mess with mascara running down my face, dressed like a hooker. A leprechaun hooker. I can't even imagine what he must think of me right now.

Duncan gets to my side and helps me out of the cab of the truck. I stumble a few times in my *ridiculous* heels, but he steadies me with a strong grip on my waist, then finally hauls me over his shoulder like a sack of potatoes. I let out a surprised yelp, but quickly settle down when I realize it's easier to let him carry me this way than to try and walk on my own. Even though my ass is hanging out.

Duncan carries me inside his home, which is surprisingly cozy and thankfully warm. He sets me down on the couch. I notice a distinct lack of feminine touches around the place. If there is a girlfriend in the picture, she's not here much.

I pull off the sweatshirt he lent me. "Thank you. I hope I didn't get mascara on it."

His eyes bug out of his head. "Jesus. Fuck. Put it back on."

"What? Why?"

"You're...I'm not supposed to...where the hell have you been hiding those curves?" He shakes his head as if to clear it. "It's cold. Keep it on."

I quickly put the sweatshirt back on, feeling self-conscious under the sudden scrutiny of his gaze. I cross my arms over my chest, trying to hide the curves he's so offended by.

Duncan seems to notice my discomfort and clears his throat. "Sorry, that was inappropriate. I just meant...you look...not like the kid I'm used to seeing. I know I saw that dress uncovered at the station, but it's even worse here."

Worse? Wow.

This night was supposed to be about bolstering my confidence, but he's just making me feel awful about myself. I take a deep breath and try to compose myself.

"I can Uber home. You don't have to be responsible for me anymore. I'm sorry that I probably ruined your St. Patrick's night."

Duncan shakes his head. "No, I can't let you go out like that. And the weather is getting worse. I wouldn't be surprised if we lose power tonight." He shakes his head again. "Those shoes look painful."

"They're not great," I admit with a grimace. "Your sister has a higher tolerance for pain than I do, I think."

Duncan sits on the coffee table in front of me and pulls my feet into his lap, undoing the straps of the heels. His fingers brush against my ankle, and it makes me shiver. I try to hide the reaction, but Duncan notices.

"Are you cold?" he asks, gesturing to the sweatshirt.

"No, I'm fine," I say quickly, trying to hide my embarrassment.

But Duncan doesn't seem convinced. He stands up and disappears into another room, leaving me alone on the couch. I hear some rustling and then he comes back, holding a blanket.

"Here, put this on," he says, draping the blanket over my legs. "I don't want you to catch a cold."

"Thank you," I say, grateful for the warmth of the blanket.

Duncan sits down next to me on the couch, leaving a safe distance between us, but I can still feel the judgment radiating off his body. I try to ignore the way my heart starts pounding in my chest because it does this whenever he's close to me. It has since I was a kid.

"So, what happened tonight?" he asks. "Why…" He gestures to my outfit. "It's not really like you."

I shrug. "That's exactly why."

"I don't understand."

"I was trying to…break out of my nerdy shell, I guess."

Duncan listens intently, his eyes fixed on me. "Why would you want to do that? You're perfect just the way you are."

I scoff. "Perfect? Right."

Duncan reaches out and takes my hand, giving it a gentle squeeze. "Trust me, you are. And anyone who can't see that is a fool."

I feel a flush rising to my cheeks at his words. No one has ever talked to me like that before. Duncan's touch is warm and reassuring, making me feel safe and protected. I lean into him, enjoying the closeness.

"There are a lot of fools at my university then."

He laughs. "Not reeling in the big fish on campus, huh?"

"Not reeling in any fish on campus. I just thought if I dressed differently, sexy, maybe tonight I could finally get noticed."

He looks me up and down and smiles. "Trust me, I think you got noticed tonight."

"Too much?"

"Yeah. That's an understatement."

"Jules said—"

He holds his hand up. "Jules is a very different girl than you are. She's my sister and I love her, but she doesn't always have the best judgment when it comes to these things."

I nod, understanding. "Jules was always the wild one, the life of the party. I was the quiet one, the nerdy one. It has always been that way."

"But you know what?" Duncan continues, his voice low and husky. "I like the nerdy you. I like the quiet you. I like the you that's sitting here next to me, wrapped up in a blanket."

I turn to face him, our faces inches apart. His eyes are a dark midnight blue and intense, causing my pulse to quicken.

Something is happening. The air is vibrating between us. His gaze lands on my lips and I can't help but lick them. A sound that could be anguish sort of chuffs out of him at the sight of my tongue.

Duncan's hand moves to my cheek, his thumb running over my bottom lip. Our breaths mingle as we stare at each other.

Duncan leans in slowly, his lips hovering over mine. I can feel his warm breath on my skin, and my heart is pounding so hard I'm sure he can hear it. And then, finally, his lips meet mine in a soft, tender kiss.

The kiss is soft at first, but quickly becomes more urgent. I feel his hand slide up my back and tangle in my hair, pulling me closer to him.

He pulls back and jumps up. "Shit. I'm sorry. I shouldn't have done that. I don't know what I was thinking. I'm so sorry, Ginger."

Four

Duncan

WHAT THE HELL WAS I thinking?

I wasn't thinking. Fuck.

I haven't been able to hold a thought in my head since she ripped off that sweatshirt and showed me how she looks in the hooker dress again. The image of all that skin is burned on my retinas.

A man is not meant to deal with this kind of temptation. I do some quick math and at least she's legal. Not drinking age legal, but she and my sister are sophomores at college now and I won't have to arrest myself.

Fuck. Fuck. Fuck.

My sister will kill me for messing with Ginger.

"You regret kissing me?" Ginger asks.

I shake my head, my eyes still glued to her lips. "No," I say slowly, drawing out the long *oh* sound. "That's not it at all."

"Then why'd you stop?" she asks, her voice barely above a whisper.

I hesitate, knowing that anything I say now will be exactly the wrong thing to say. There's no right thing. I've made an impossibly bad situation worse.

"I stopped because I don't want to do anything that would hurt Jules," I say, trying to keep my voice steady. It's only half the truth, but it's the part that I can say out loud without feeling like a complete asshole.

Ginger nods, her eyes downcast. "I understand," she says, but I don't think she does. She's taking this personally, and after what she told me about not finding dates, I can see why.

The wind howls outside, ice pellets hitting the windows as the power flickers.

"It's not that I don't find you attractive," I say.

"Please. Stop. I don't want to have this conversation. I've had enough mortification tonight."

"Ginger..."

She holds her hand up. "May I use your bathroom please?"

I nod, watching her walk away with a heavy heart. I've messed this up royally. I shouldn't have kissed her, shouldn't have let myself get carried away like that. I know better. But the truth is, I'm attracted to her. More than I should be. More than I'm comfortable with.

And her wearing my sweatshirt and walking around my house barefoot is not helping. The fact that my shirt hangs past the hem of her skirt is not lost on me either.

But then I hear the bathroom door open and Ginger's footsteps approaching. I turn around and my breath catches in my throat.

Ginger looks like herself again with her fresh washed face and glasses replacing what must have been contacts. But she's holding the little green scrap of a dress, which means she's nearly naked under my shirt. Maybe actually naked because I didn't see any bra straps or panty lines at the station, and I was looking pretty hard.

She's still covered a hundred times more than she was in that dress, but her naked body under my shirt is more erotic than anything I've ever seen.

And the glasses. They're huge and not very attractive, but somehow turn me unreasonably the fuck on. Like, now that I've seen the vixen version of my sister's best friend, the OG reminder has somehow become hot. So fucking hot.

"I'm sorry," she says quietly, her eyes meeting mine for a brief moment before she turns away.

I take a deep breath, trying to steady my racing heart. "For what?" I ask, my voice coming out gruff.

"For making you uncomfortable."

I shake my head. "You don't have to apologize. I'm the one who should be sorry. I shouldn't have kissed you."

Ginger hesitates for a moment before nodding. "It's okay," she says. "It's just... this was a mistake, wasn't it?"

I take a step towards her and nod. "Yes, it was," I say. "But that doesn't mean it wasn't a good mistake."

She smiles shyly and heat blooms in my chest. Oh man, this is bad. A transformer could have less electricity running through it than I have right now. Forcing myself to turn away, I walk back toward the kitchen and she follows silently.

"Are you hungry? I have—"

The room is thrust into darkness, and she runs into my back. I turn to steady her, my hands grasping her maybe too tightly.

"You okay?"

"Not a big fan of the dark, actually."

I can feel her body trembling against mine, and my protective instincts kick in. "Don't worry, I've got you," I say, trying to keep my voice steady. I pull Ginger into an embrace, soothing my hand down her back as she clings to me. In the darkness, I can hear her breathing quicken, and I know that I have to do something to distract her.

"If you hadn't got arrested for hooking tonight, what would you be doing right now?"

She laughs. "I'd probably be back in my dorm room reading."

"Not in that dress."

"No, I would have taken it off and put on my ratty pajamas."

"No, I mean, you would be with someone. The way you looked in that dress tonight. You would have had them fighting over you."

She laughs again, as if the image of another man touching her isn't doing serious damage to my stomach lining. "I wouldn't have gone home with anyone. I'd have chickened out. I always do."

I should be getting the flashlight and the emergency lights out. Starting a fire in the wood stove. But the dark is creating an intimate space to talk, like we're not part of the real world anymore. "Why do you chicken out?"

"I'm too nervous to hook up. I get shy and weird and say the wrong things. I always think the guy's going to think I'm stupid or boring or something. I'm not like other girls. I don't know how to be sexy."

She speaks with a mix of embarrassment and self-doubt. I want to tell her how wrong she is, that she's the sexiest woman I've ever seen. But I know she wouldn't believe me, so instead I just tighten my arms around her and whisper, "You don't have to be anyone but yourself."

"You keep saying that, but myself isn't who guys want."

She's so wrong about that. "You're hanging out with the wrong guys."

Before I do anything stupid, I break up the hug and pull my phone from my pocket and use the flashlight on it. Keeping her hand in mine, we walk across the kitchen to the junk drawer, where I pull out two actual flashlights.

"See, I told you I'd take care of you," I say, handing her one of the flashlights.

"Thanks," she says, a small smile tugging at the corner of her lips.

I set up a battery-operated lantern in the kitchen and have her start to forage for snacks while I go build a fire and set up a nest of blankets in the living room.

When she is settled, I go change into joggers and hurry back to our nest. The house is already getting cold.

"I brought you a pair of wool socks."

"Sexy," she says.

Just the word on her lips makes me sweat. I laugh and offer her the socks. She slides them on and then I wrap us up in a blanket.

"Why didn't you go out tonight?" she asks me.

"I hate bars. I'm happier at home."

"Same."

"Yet you were out. Going to a crowded bar where everyone was drinking very ill-advised green beer and talking like drunk leprechauns."

"I'm never going to lose my...find a guy...if I stay home all the time."

It's like she dropped a bomb in my living room. She didn't have to say it. I understood the left-out word as clearly as if she had shouted it at the top of her lungs.

My little prostitute is a virgin.

Five

———

Ginger

I CAN'T BELIEVE I ALMOST told Duncan I was a virgin.

I'm such an awkward mess.

"What kind of guy are you looking for?" he asks.

I think of all the things I'd put on my fictitious dating app profile and realize he'd be the perfect guy for me. If he wasn't my best friend's older brother. If he hadn't watched me grow up through my even more than current awkward phase.

And there's no way he could be the guy to get me out of my head. I'd be way too nervous to lose control around him. No, my "perfect guy" will have to be a stranger.

"Ginger?" he prods. "What kind of guy?"

"Sorry. Spaced out. Um. I don't know if I have a type or anything. Not a frat bro. That much I know."

He laughs. "Hey, I was a frat bro."

"No way. I mean, I guess I knew you were a jock in school. But I can't picture you acting like...they are hideous. I can't even imagine you hanging out with them, let alone being one of them. And those houses are disgusting. Did you live in one of those houses?"

"Well, to be honest, I wasn't really a stereotypical frat bro. I just wanted to play football and party a little. But I get what you mean. They can be pretty obnoxious. And I sure as hell always wore shoes in the house."

He laughs and I can't help but smile. "Yeah, that's a must," I agree. "So, what kind of guy do you think I should look for?"

"Someone thoughtful and kind," he says without hesitation. "Someone who respects your boundaries and appreciates your intelligence and wit."

I roll my eyes. Hard. "You sound like a parent character on a family cable channel. One of those very special episodes."

"Do I? I guess I do. Someone who's smart enough to keep up with you then. Which is a tall order. Someone who puts you first. Someone not a frat bro, I see that now. At least not a stereotypical frat bro."

I feel my cheeks heat up. Is he describing himself or is this just wishful thinking on my part?

"That sounds like the perfect guy," I say, trying to keep my voice steady. We sit in silence for a moment, wrapped up in the blanket.

"So, what about you?" I ask, trying to change the subject. "Are you dating someone?"

The fire crackles. "Not for a while. Single. I'm single a lot, actually."

Which makes no sense to me. He's handsome, kind, funny. He has a nice house and a good job. And he can be talked out of his occasional chauvinism pretty easily.

"What kind of woman are you looking for then?"

He shrugs. "I don't really know. Someone who's smart, funny, drama free."

What he's not saying is blonde, model thin, former cheerleader, and sexy. That's what most guys are looking for. But I'm none of those things. I'm just plain, boring Ginger. The strange friend of his little sister.

I can tell he's trying to be polite and not offend me with his answer, but it stings a little. To know I'm not his type.

But then he turns to me, his eyes catching the light from the candles through the darkness. "Actually, there is one more thing I'm looking for in a woman."

"What's that?" I ask, intrigued.

"Someone who wants a dog."

Okay, I was not expecting that. "Why don't you just get a dog if you want one?"

"I work long hours sometimes. It wouldn't be fair to a dog to be alone that much. But if I had a girlfriend who loved me and loved our dog, then she and the dog could keep each other company." He shakes his head. "My last date hated dogs."

"What kind of person hates dogs?"

"Right?"

A strong gust of wind rattles the windows. But we're so warm and cozy under the blanket that the sound just makes me feel toastier. Safer. We continue talking about dogs for a while, and I can't help but notice how much he lights up when talking about them. It's adorable.

As the fire dies down, he stands up and stretches. "While I put more wood on the fire, why don't you tell me why you're still a virgin."

I inhale sharply at the abrupt change of subject. So he figured that out from our previous conversation after all. I thought I covered myself by not saying it. "Actually, I don't think that is any of your business.

"Fair enough," he says, grabbing some logs from the pile and tossing them onto the fire. "I didn't mean to pry."

"Yes you did."

"Yes I did. It's the detective in me I guess. I mean, my sister is your best friend, and she lost her virginity in what...tenth grade?"

"Eighth."

"No shit? Eighth grade? Wow."

"I'm surprised you didn't know. She stole the condoms from your room."

He laughs, shaking his head in disbelief. "I guess I shouldn't be surprised. That girl has always been wild. But eighth grade is...she didn't get taken advantage of by an older guy, did she? Not like I can do anything about it now, but..."

"No. He was in our grade. He was really nice, actually. They thought they were in love for six whole weeks. Which is probably her longest relationship. But I'm pretty sure going all the way was her idea, not his."

Duncan looks relieved. "So again...how is it that my sister is...well, you know how Jules is...and you are...not."

I shrug, feeling a little uncomfortable with the topic. "I'm not brave like her. I guess I just haven't found the right person yet. It all kind of scares me, being intimate with someone."

He looks at me intently. "Did somebody hurt you?"

"No, nothing like that. I didn't start out afraid of sex. I was just so awkward for most of my teen years, as I'm sure you remember." He politely declines to agree verbally. "And then when I finally started figuring out how to be at least a little less weird, I waited too long and now it's like this thing that's bigger than I am. Like some big anxious brain thing. So I keep trying to...this is embarrassing."

"No, I want to hear."

"I keep trying to find a guy who can make me stop thinking."

He stares at me for a beat too long, his gaze making me squirm a little. "You're asking a lot from a mortal, you know. You have a supercomputer brain. A guy would have to be pretty confident about himself to think he can get you out of your head."

I shrug. "I know."

As he sits back down next to me, the fire crackles and pops, filling the room with warmth. He takes a deep breath, as if he's about to say something important. Then doesn't say a word.

"What were you about to say?" I ask.

"It's not scary. Sex. It can be a lot of different things. Sometimes intense. Sometimes hilarious. But I wish you wouldn't build it up as some huge scary thing."

I wish the same thing.

Duncan's words resonate with me, but it's hard to shake off the anxiety that's been a part of me for so long. "I know you're right. I just can't help feeling like I'm missing out on something important. Everyone else seems to have it figured out."

"Everyone is just pretending to have it figured out," he says with a wry smile. "Trust me. People are always more insecure than they let on. And as for missing out...well, I think you're missing out on a lot more by not letting yourself experience intimacy in some way or another."

I nod, taking in his words. Maybe he's right. Maybe I'm putting too much pressure on myself to have everything figured out. Duncan seems so self-assured and confident, but if even he has his moments of doubt and insecurity...

"I get to a certain point with a guy and then...I just can't stop overthinking."

Duncan nods in understanding. "It's normal to have those thoughts, but it's important not to let them consume you. You have to learn how to let go and just be in the moment. It's not easy, but the more you do it, the easier it becomes."

I take a deep breath, feeling a weight lifted off my shoulders. Maybe it's not as scary as I thought.

"You make it sound so simple."

"It's not simple, but it's not impossible either."

We stop talking and watch the flames in the little window of his wood stove for a few minutes.

He exhales on a whistle. "I could make you come."

Six

Duncan

I CAN'T BELIEVE I JUST told Ginger I could make her come.

What the hell is wrong with me? That would be wrong on so many levels. She's my little sister's best friend. She's still in college. She's a *virgin*.

But I'm not wrong. I could make her come.

"Duncan," she whispers, her eyes big and round. "I can't ask you to do that."

I stifle a chuckle. "It's not a hardship to make a pretty woman come. It's like the best thing ever."

"But you don't...I'm not your type."

Ginger has no idea how hard I've been since I saw her in that dress tonight.

I can do this. I can help her with her anxiety. I won't take her virginity though. I can't even let her see my cock or she'll go deer in the headlights on me and lose whatever ground we gain on her fear.

I've seen the look enough to know.

"You're absolutely my type," I tell her, my voice low and husky. "And I'm absolutely going to make you come."

"I'm feeling really embarrassed right now. What if I can't shut my mind off? What do we tell Jules? What—"

I put my hand over her lips. "Do you trust me?"

She nods. God, I *love* that. She trusts me.

I reach behind and pull my shirt off. The little whimper she lets out is gratifying.

"You tell me to stop whenever you need to and I will."

She nods again.

I pull the blanket off her legs. "We don't have to tell anyone about this. It's just for us, okay? All you have to do is try to relax and I will do the rest. I have a theory that the guys you've tried to be intimate with are very nice, very respectful young men. Like one of those family channel characters you mentioned earlier. Am I right?"

"Yes."

I grab her calves and slide her flat onto her back, causing a little yelp. "I'm not as nice. Spread your legs."

Instead, she bites her lip and looks at me nervously.

"I thought you said you trusted me."

She spreads her legs, showing me the treasure between them.

"Good girl." I caress her thighs. I was right. No panties.

I get between her legs and inhale her sweet scent before giving her a soft kiss right there.

She gasps and her hips rock instinctively.

Ginger needs a man who will dominate her enough to keep her focus on her body. I'm going to be that man for tonight.

I slide my tongue along her slit and she arches her back, letting out a moan. I continue my exploration, alternating between soft and hard licks until she is trembling and panting.

"You taste so good, Ginger. I fucking love eating your pussy."

She moans. "Oh my God. I can't believe…oh…nobody has ever…oh…"

She's so wet. I can't get enough of her. I increase the tempo of my tongue, pushing her closer and closer to the edge. Then I focus on her clit, which drives her into a frenzy. She wraps her legs around my neck, and I feel her quivering against my face. More of her juices flow, and I lap them up hungrily.

So fucking good. I could live here, between her legs.

When she comes, it's like a wave of pleasure that engulfs her entire body. She floods my mouth with her orgasm, and I revel in the taste of her bliss.

When she finally comes down from her orgasm, she looks into my eyes with a mixture of shock and awe. "Wow."

"Not done with you."

"I don't think I can…"

I pull her up to sitting and pull off the sweatshirt she's wearing before laying her back down. "Wasn't asking."

I dip my fingers back through her folds and gather the slick wet, using my fingers to paint one of her nipples. I latch onto it hungrily, slurping her girl cum from her tits.

"Oh God. That's…that seems so naughty."

I grin and nip her breast. "I never claimed to be a Boy Scout."

I move down her body, licking and kissing every inch of her until I reach her thighs. She gasps as I slip my tongue back inside her, pushing her to the edge again.

"I'm going to make you come so hard," I whisper against her skin.

Ginger's hips buck wildly as I lick and suck her, pushing her closer and closer to the edge. When she finally comes, her entire body trembles and she cries out my name, the name of several deities, some nonsense words, and finally just some little kitten mewls that make me prouder than the day I graduated from academy.

I feel her cum dripping down my chin. Her fingers are in my hair, and I rest my head on her abdomen until she's breathing normally again.

I'm hard as a fucking brick. I don't think I've ever wanted to come more than I do right now. But...virgin. She's not for me.

Not for the guy who went by "Horse" all throughout high school and college.

I press a kiss to her navel. "You're very responsive, GinGin. That was amazing."

A breath shudders through her. "That was more than amazing. Are we still going to...I want to keep going. If you want."

I wish that were a possibility.

"I want. I very much want." But I can't. "I think it's best if we stop here, though."

She raises up on her elbows. "I think that is the opposite of best. Why don't you want to have sex with me?"

"Ginger, I do want to have sex with you. But..."

"But what?"

"I'm too big." Her brow is furrowed in confusion, so I put her hand on my cock and let her feel the bat between my legs. "*It's* too big."

Her eyes widen. "Oh. That's...that's a lot."

I nod. "It's too much."

Ginger's eyes soften. "It can't be too much. Women were made to—"

"Very few women have been able to...take me. I don't want to hurt you. I don't want to hurt anyone. But your first time shouldn't be with a freak."

"Oh my God, Duncan. You are not a freak. You're well endowed is all. The physics of the situation say my body can accommodate you."

"I'm glad you are up on your science, but 'can' and 'should' are two different things."

"At least let me see it."

"Ginger..."

"Please. I want to see it. I want to know what I'm missing out on."

One girl in college cried when she saw it. She asked if I was a porn star. And I guess if law enforcement hadn't worked out, I could have tried my luck in the adult entertainment business. But it really isn't my style.

"Please," she asks. "I really want to know. For science."

I shake my head, but I can't deny Ginger anything. "You're infuriating, but fine. But don't say I didn't warn you." I stand and take off my joggers, standing over her so she can get a long hard look at my long, hard dick.

Seven

—

Ginger

IT TAKES ME A MINUTE for my mind and my eyes to agree on what we are seeing.

Duncan is bigger than anything I could have expected. I've seen some pretty big ones, not in real life, but still. The man in front of me is a giant. "How…do you have to get your pants specially made?"

"No," he answers without humor. In fact, he seems very guarded.

"How big is it?"

"I've never measured."

Now he's just being surly.

"That is a lie. How big is it?"

"A bit more than average."

"Duncan," I warn.

"Nine." He waits a bit. "And a quarter." He looks up at the ceiling like it's his biggest failing. Big being the operative word. "It's the girth that gives me the most trouble. Gives women the most trouble, I mean. Are you done?"

"No. May I touch it?"

He lets out a restrained groan. "Not a good idea."

From what I understand about guys, which I admit isn't a lot, this penis in front of me is the holy grail of penises. Why isn't he proud of it?

"Why aren't you walking around town swinging this at anyone who will look at it?

The look he shoots me could peel paint. "It's not something to be proud of. I was born with it, just like some people are born with six toes or a third nipple. And it's caused me more problems than anything else in my life."

I'm not sure I understand. How could having a giant penis be a problem? It sounds like a dream come true. But looking at the guarded expression on Duncan's face, I know not he doesn't see it that way.

"Why is it a problem?"

"Because it's too big. It can be uncomfortable for me and...it can be uncomfortable for women, too. Sometimes painful." And judging from the clenched jaw, he's uncomfortable with this conversation.

"I see. Duncan, please look at me."

He does. "I'm not scared. I'm not intimidated. I'm not even slightly freaked out. I'm intrigued, and curious, and I want to know what it feels like."

"For a smart girl, you're not thinking clearly."

"Ouch."

He pinches the bridge of his nose. "I'm sorry. I shouldn't have said that. I think I should put my pants back on now."

"I wish you wouldn't. I don't think we're done."

"We should be. You're a virgin. They call me Horse. It's not the recipe for a gentle initiation. You should be locking yourself in the bathroom and crying."

"Oh my God. Has that happened to you?"

"Twice."

I'm guessing a guy with a micro-penis probably has more to complain about than a guy with...*that*. But I can tell that the very thing that should give him more confidence has somehow done the opposite. I reach out and touch his arm. "It's part of you. It's big, yes. But it's not like it has a mind of its own and it's going to tackle me to the floor."

He laughs like he doesn't mean to let the chuckle out. "It does actually have a mind of its own. And if you touch it, I might tackle you to the floor with it. I'm on the edge here, GinGin. I shouldn't have let us get this far."

I get up on my knees. Eye level with his cock.

Wow.

It's really something. The flared tip is leaking precum. I want to rub him all over my face. Is that normal? I want to taste him there, the way he tasted me. My jaw hurts thinking about it, but I want to try just the same.

My body is humming, and I know I'm ready for something. Not ready like I was at the beginning of the night when I hoped to just find someone to break my hymen.

I want something more. I want Duncan.

I take a deep breath and place my hands on Duncan's hips. His muscles twitch beneath my touch. But he hasn't given me permission to touch his cock, and so I will wait until he does.

He's looming over me, his masculine body so powerful. His scent is musky and earthy, and I want to lick him from head to toe. Yet despite his obvious strength, despite my position on the floor, despite my inexperience and naivete, it dawns on me that I have all the power at this moment. Me, little geeky Ginger still wearing her dorky glasses and Duncan's wool socks, but nothing else.

I want him from a place inside me that has nothing to do with my anxious desires to finally catch a boy to deflower me. Instead, I want him from a place that recognizes this man is different from all the others. This man is made for me in a way that no one else can ever be.

I have *always* wanted him.

I slide my hands up and down his tree trunk thighs, feeling the muscles ripple beneath my touch. I look into his eyes and see the desire burning in them. He's watching me intently, looking at me with almost possessive intent.

"Oh, Duncan," I sigh. "I want you so much."

He groans and grabs my wrist, guiding my hand around his aforementioned girth, my fingers unable to encircle him completely.

His cock is amazing. He pulses in my hand, soft velvety flesh over hard steel. I can feel the blood rushing through him, the power, the need.

I start to stroke him, up and down. His breathing gets heavier, and he's somehow getting impossibly harder. The dripping precum gives me some lubrication, so I use one hand to roll the tip over my palm to get it wet.

When he growls like an animal at me, I pause.

"Do you want me to stop?" I whisper.

He shakes his head, his eyes closed, his breathing ragged. "That was so fucking hot."

Whew. "Do you want me to go faster?"

He nods, his grip tightening on my wrist.

I can feel my own body responding, heat pooling between my thighs and my nipples pebbling as he uses my hand to masturbate. When I catch his rhythm, he lets go and wraps his hand in my hair.

I add my other hand, stroking him with both. There's so much of him. And all of it pleases me.

He's pushing back against my hands now, his hips rocking in time with my strokes. His cock grows somehow even bigger, and I know he's close. I want his orgasm as badly as I wanted my own not that long ago.

The secrets of being a woman, a sexual woman, that have eluded me for so long become clearer with every stroke of my hand.

He grabs my shoulder, his grip probably bruising, and pulls me closer, his hips bucking. His mouth falls open and his eyes roll back as his orgasm takes over. Warmth spills onto my skin as he empties himself.

I keep going, milking him until every last drop is released.

Duncan sinks to his knees onto the floor with me and wraps me into a hug. His breathing is still heavy, and his body is trembling.

We stay like that for a long while, until his breathing evens out.

"Fuck. Jules is going to kill us," he finally says.

"You better not let me die a virgin, Duncan O'Malley."

"Ginger...we've already done too much. I can't...it wouldn't be right."

"You will. And it will be better than just right. You know it will. You know we're going to do it. Let's stop fighting and just accept it."

He puts his face in the crook of my neck and breathes me in. "We'll take a break. If you still want to after that. I'm tired of fighting you."

Eight

Duncan

NAKED GIN RUMMY BY candlelight is surprisingly fun. I like the way it feels like we are the only two people on the planet. And if that were true, I think we'd do okay. As hot as I am for Ginger, I also really like her. She's been around as long as I can remember, but I've never really gotten to know her as more than my sister's best friend. She's funny and smart.

And she tastes good.

Immediately, thoughts of her sweet pussy crowd my mind, and my mouth starts watering. I try to focus on the game again, but the tension between us is growing thicker. And so am I.

Break time is over. For better or worse. She shouldn't be here with me like this, but I'm having a hard time regretting it.

"Wanna make out?" I ask her.

"Yes!" She throws her cards over her shoulder. "I'm probably not very good at it. But yes."

She's so damned cute and enthusiastic. I'm not worried about her skill level by any means. She picked up on the hand job pretty fucking fast. And she's been very responsive to everything we've done together. Kissing her is going to be amazing.

We scoot closer under the blanket when I take her mouth. My tongue slides inside hers instantly, tasting her and exploring. My hands wander down her body, cupping her ass and kneading it.

Need to slow this down or we're going to catch fire.

I pull away, leaving her breathless. Grasping her chin in my hand, I tell her, "You kiss me like you've been kissing me your whole life. I can't get enough of you."

I nuzzle her neck, sending a flurry of goose bumps across her skin. So that's an erogenous zone for her. Good to know. I spend some time there, exploring and teasing her. Smelling her hair.

I got it bad.

Her moans are like music. I'm barely able to contain my own arousal, I'm so close to the edge. But I don't want to rush this.

I pull away, giving her a gentle kiss on the lips.

"Am I squishing you?" I ask.

"No. I like the weight of you on me." She runs her hands over my body. Her touch is gentle and slow. I close my eyes and savor the sensations. I'm not sure what she's thinking, but I can tell she's enjoying it.

I'm in good physical shape, I have to be for my job. But I'm not cut like diamonds. I'm healthy, but I've got a dad bod for sure. My buddy told me women like it. It makes them feel safe and comfortable.

Ginger seems to like it. I roll to my side so she can explore me some more. Her tiny hands delve through my chest hair and lower to my belly. I'm hairy there too, not much for manscaping. She makes this little cooing sound that lifts my cock even more. I'm probably going to come again before I get anywhere near inside her.

"I really like the way you feel," she murmurs.

Jesus. My chest puffs up like I'm some kind of sex god just because she likes touching my stomach.

Her hand brushes against my cock and I hiss.

"Sorry," she says. "Should I not have…"

"Baby, you're fine. I'm just really close. Maybe let me touch you for a while?"

She nods.

I move slowly and deliberately, taking my time to explore her body. My hands caress her curves and my lips follow close behind. I kiss and tease her neck, her breasts, her belly, and her inner thighs.

The scent of her arousal is intoxicating as fuck.

I slide my hand up her stomach, circling her nipples. I take her mouth again, my body shifting over hers, pressing her into the nest we made of blankets. My hand comes between us, circling her clit until she's pushing up to meet me, rubbing herself on my very hard cock. She's so wet.

Her hands slide down my back, her nails lightly scratching my skin. I moan into her mouth as my cock jumps, wanting her. She wraps her legs around my hips.

"Please, Duncan."

I sit back on my knees and thump my heavy cock on her pussy. "I get tested regularly, but I haven't been with anyone since I broke up with my ex in January."

"Um, okay," she answers like she has no idea why I'm telling her this. Since she's very smart, I'm going to take credit for her befuddled mind. "I'm clean," I explain. "No diseases. Which you should have asked me about before you let my cock go anywhere near your pussy. Are you on birth control?"

Her brain starts to catch up. "Yes. I've been trying to lose my virginity for a year, so I'm on birth control."

That's good, though I don't like being reminded that she's been actively looking for a man to do to her what I want to do to her. More of my patriarchal bullshit coming through as jealousy about phantom men she might have fucked when she wasn't even in my orbit.

"I have condoms in my room. But that requires I get up and leave this hot, hot pussy." I slide my cock through her folds and we both shudder. "Do you want me to get one? It's okay if you do."

"I trust you're telling me the truth about being tested."

As good as that feels to hear, I also feel very protective of her. "You should never trust a guy who tells you that."

She laughs at my attempt to scold her while I'm rubbing her pussy with my cock. "I've known you my whole life, Duncan. I trust you."

I shake my head. "A guy will say anything to get pussy. Even the nice guys."

I should go get the condoms anyway. And lube. But she's so fucking wet already, I don't think we will need it. And I don't want to leave her. I don't know if I physically can. My body is aching to be inside her.

Aching.

I notch myself at her entrance, but it's a tight fit. The sight of the head of my cock breaching that little hole is obscenely hot. I can't resist pushing in a little just a little more, moaning as I feel her body clench around me.

I pull out and dip my fingers into her pussy for her natural lubrication to spread over myself.

I can't believe how wet this girl is as I paint it all over my cock. Fuck if rubbing her all over me isn't hot.

Slowly, never more aware that I'm too fucking thick to put myself inside this girl, I push in just a little.

She holds her breath.

"You okay?"

She squeaks.

"Breathe, Ginger."

She takes a deep breath and I push further.

"Good girl."

"That's just the tip, isn't it?"

"Yeah, I'm afraid so."

Nine

Ginger

IT'S FIRE DOWN THERE. The stretch feels unlike anything I've ever felt. Duncan doesn't move, just lets me get used to the invasion of his body in mine. I'm scared and aroused all at once. His tenderness helps me relax, but I'm still so anxious.

He pushes in a little more and I gasp. He pauses, making sure I'm okay.

"Just a little more, Ginger."

We both know that's a lie.

This is the furthest I've gone with a guy, and I was so ready. But now, I'm starting to feel a little claustrophobic or something. Can you be claustrophobic from the inside?

His hand strokes my hip, and I can feel the tension of his muscles as he works to control himself. All that power, the masculine energy that radiates off him, wraps around me. He could do anything he wants to me, but he won't.

"Ginger, I need you to just relax, okay? You're so tight."

I try to do as he says, trying to relax my muscles. Little by little, I feel him stretch me and take me further. But I think I'm going to screw this up. I'm not going to be able to have sex tonight after all. Am I still a virgin or have I gone too far?

"Can you do something for me, GinGin?"

I can hardly breathe, but sure. Whatever. "What?"

"Can you recite the *Periodic Table of Elements*?"

What now? I'm trying not to overthink, or think at all, and he wants me to think *more*?

"Duncan?" Has he lost his mind? Why would I want to do that? Is this some kind of kink I don't know about?

"For me. Just try."

I close my eyes.

"Hydrogen. Helium. Lithium. Beryllium. Boron...Carbon. Nitrogen. Oxy...oxygen. Fluorine. Ne-Neon..."

And as I recite, Duncan inches himself further into my body. I'm so distracted that I almost don't realize what's happening. Almost. But as I keep going, focusing as hard as I can. I can feel that he's in deeper now.

And suddenly, I'm filled with him.

"Oh my God," I say, in awe. "Did I do it? All the way?"

"To the root," he replies, then starts kissing my neck, holding himself still below the waist. "Such a good fucking girl."

Oh. *Ohhh*. My inner muscles tense up around him on the praise. He huffs a laugh in my hair and pulls back to look me in the eye.

"I think I liked it when you called me a good girl."

"I'm going to have to agree with you on that. Let's find out what else you like."

Duncan rocks his hips, and I gasp so he pauses.

"I'm okay. Good gasp, I swear."

He's still not moving a lot down below, but he kisses down my chest and lands on my nipples, drawing one deeply into his mouth. I feel it directly in my clit, like they are connected by a wire, and I can't help but arch my back. Wrapping my legs around his big body opens me up even more.

Duncan's breathing is getting heavier, his heart beating faster against my chest. The wiry hair there and on his belly is hot in a very primal way. He slowly moves his hips, creating a gentle rhythm, and I let out a low moan. He increases the speed very slowly, and I know it must be costing him so much to go slow.

He builds me up until I'm clinging to him, and when I'm about to break, he slows down and starts again, taking me higher and higher.

"You feel so good on my cock, Ginger."

"I've never felt better in my entire life."

He rests his forehead against mine and stops moving. "I'm very close, but I need you to come first." His thumb goes to my clit, brushing it gently. "Are you going to want me to pull out when it's time?"

"God no."

He closes his eyes. "You want me to fill your little pussy with cum, naughty girl?"

His words and more pressure on my clit send me into an upward spiral. "Yes. Fuck yes."

"You've been taking my cock so good. You deserve whatever you want."

"I want you to come inside me." And I do. I feel like I was made for him to come inside me. I knew I wanted to experience sex because it was supposed to feel good, but now it feels like a biological imperative for him to release into me.

"I will. But first you need to come. Can you do that for me, pretty girl? Can you come on my cock?" He picks up my ass, canting my hips slightly. The new angle creates an even more intense sensation. One that steals my breath.

"Yes, yes, oh God, yes!" I come hard, my body shaking against his.

"Jesus, look at you. So pretty when you come."

My whole body is quaking with pleasure unlike anything I've ever even imagined. My nails are scoring his shoulders, and I'm probably speaking in tongues.

And then, more than anything, I need Duncan to come inside me. "Oh God. Duncan fill me up with your cum. Please. Fill me up."

He grunts and thrusts hard into me, vibrating against my walls. His body tenses and he comes with a roar, his grip tightening around me. Hot cum spills inside me, and I'm coming again, my orgasm overlapping with his.

He collapses on top of me, both of us panting and sweaty, and I feel closer to him than I have to anyone in my life.

When he makes to pull out, I dig my heels into his ass. "Not yet."

"Ginger, you must be sore."

"I'm not ready to let you go."

Which is probably the wrong thing to say since this is probably a one-time thing.

I'm so embarrassed. Why must I always be so awkward?

Duncan brushes my bangs off my glasses. I can't believe I'm still wearing my glasses. My God. What is *wrong* with me?

He kisses my nose. "I'm not going anywhere."

Ten

Duncan

IN A LITTLE WHILE, I am sure I will be filled with remorse and regret for what I've done, taking the virginity of my little sister's best friend. But right now, it's hard to feel anything but elation.

That was the most erotic experience of my life. I can't believe I didn't tear her in two, but little Ginger, so tight and wet and responsive, took every damn inch. And loved it.

I want nothing more than to stay inside her, to be a part of her. I never want to leave her.

But I know I must.

I kiss her forehead and pull out slowly. Ginger is still trembling from her orgasm, and I feel a deep satisfaction knowing I fucking rocked her world as much as she rocked mine.

"I'll be right back," I tell her and go into the bathroom, hoping there's still enough hot water to wet down a cloth. I bring it back out, luke warm. "I want to clean you. Will you let me?"

"Um. You don't have to," she says. "It's kind of embarrassing. You know, being taken care of like that."

"I want to," I say firmly. I cup her chin in my hand and kiss her deeply. Then I take the cloth and gently clean her sweet pussy.

When I'm done, I kiss her again and tuck her under the covers. Ginger snuggles against me, her body still trembling.

"Thank you," she whispers.

I don't know what for, but I don't ask. I just kiss her forehead and hold her until she falls asleep. I drift off, waking when the lights all come on at once. Power is back.

Ginger groans and pulls the blankets over her head.

I get up and stoke the fire and turn off the unnecessary lights. I'm too keyed up to go back to sleep. What am I going to do with this woman now? I took her virginity for fuck's sake. She should be with some young college guy, not an older man like me. Six years seems like a lot when she's only twenty.

But what I regret the most is that I don't regret it. She turns me on. A lot. It's hard to believe I hardly noticed her until last night.

And she took me. All of me. Most of the women I've been with just *can't*. My last girlfriend and I didn't have intercourse very often. She gave me a lot of handjobs, but would rarely take me in her pussy or mouth. It was too uncomfortable for her.

So how did the little sleeping pixie next to me manage to get my whole cock stuffed inside her?

I sigh and look at the clock. It's 4:30 in the morning. I should try and get some more sleep. I crawl back into bed and wrap my arms around Ginger's warm body. She sighs contentedly and cuddles closer.

A couple hours later, I wake up to find her staring at me.

"Hey." She smiles shyly.

"Hey." I return the smile.

"Thank you," she says again.

"For what?"

"For everything. Last night was amazing. I never expected it."

I laugh and kiss her forehead. "I worried you might wake up regretting me."

"I'm going to be sore for a week, and I think some of my organs are out of place, but I don't regret you at all."

I wince. "I'm sorry, baby. Do you want to take a bath? If the water heater isn't up to it, I can boil you some water to fill the tub."

"That sounds nice, but I'd like to make you breakfast first."

"You don't have to cook for me."

"I'm starving," she answers. "And I make the best pancakes."

A memory from our shared past rings a bell. "That's right. I remember you and Jules in the kitchen Sunday mornings. You did make the best pancakes. What was her job?"

"Juice. That's still all she can make. I never get to cook in the dorm. You don't mind?"

"Baby, you can make whatever you want."

I take a quick shower and when I come out, I follow my nose to the kitchen. Bacon and coffee.

Ginger is wearing my sweatshirt and those wooly socks I gave her. And the fucking hot glasses, of course. She's concentrating on stirring the batter, so I watch her for a minute, amazed at how much I like seeing her in my kitchen, in my clothes. The area around my heart feels fuzzy.

"Good morning," I say, heading to the coffee pot. "Smells good in here."

Ginger turns and smiles. "I'm just about to cook the pancakes. Pour me a cup? Cream, please."

I bring it to her, setting it next to the stove. I can't stop myself from wrapping my arms around her and nuzzling into the back of her neck. She leans her head back onto my shoulder.

"This is nice," she says, resting in my arms.

"Yeah, it is," I answer, kissing her neck softly.

We stand there for a few moments, just enjoying each other. Then she pulls away and flips the first pancake. I grab the bacon and get out the plates.

While we're eating, her phone buzzes. "Jules," she tells me. "What should I tell her?"

"What do you want to tell her?"

She sends a message and goes back to her pancakes.

"What did you say?" I ask, curious.

"I told her you would bring me home soon if the roads were okay. That we weathered out the storm here."

"Are you going to tell her about us?" I ask.

"Should I?"

"Do you want to?"

"Do you want me to?"

This conversation is getting us nowhere. It's obvious that both of us want to know what the other one is thinking without having to say it first.

"Just because I'm older than you doesn't make me more mature," I say.

"I'm well aware of that, Duncan." Her tone is sarcastic, but her eyes are sparkling under her glasses.

"Fine. Last night was amazing, but it shouldn't have happened."

Her face falls, and I feel like a jerk.

"But I'm glad it did. Ginger, I know you were just hoping to find someone to lose your virginity to last night, and I wasn't your first choice. And I know that my sister is your very best friend, and she will probably not be happy to share you with me. And I know I'm old and boring and a cop...but maybe we could try going on a date or two to see if this is something..." I take a big drink of coffee to distract myself from whatever she says next.

"You want to take me on a date?"

I nod.

She stares at her plate, dragging her fork through the leftover syrup. "I've never been on a date."

"What now?" That can't be possible. I knew she was a virgin before last night, but never been on a date? Is every man in the world an idiot?

"I haven't had much of a chance," she says. "Most guys my age don't even know I exist."

She looks so sad and vulnerable that I can't help but pull her into a hug on my lap. God she feels so good. Like she was made for me in every way.

"It's okay," I whisper into her hair. "We'll take it slow. I'll be your first."

She smiles and snuggles closer, and I can feel my heart beginning to beat faster. We sit like that for a few moments until she pulls away and looks up at me.

"Duncan, if you're too nice to me, I will get the wrong idea, I guarantee it. Dating and sex are a different language to me. Sometimes I take things too literally with people, and I misunderstand. I can see it being a hundred times worse after being intimate with someone, so you're going to have to be very clear or I will have us in an imaginary fairy tale romance when you mean to be fuck buddies who go the movies sometimes."

I squeeze her thigh. "I will be very clear. I promise."

"Okay," she nods. "So you want to take me on a couple of dates. I'm assuming you will want to have sex also?"

"Yes to the sex for sure. Also, I'd like us to be exclusive," I tell her.

She widens her eyes. "I didn't think fuck buddies did that, but okay. That's good, right? Easier to stay healthy. Okay."

"Also, I'd prefer you call me your boyfriend than your fuck buddy."

"My boyfriend?" she repeats as if I'd just told her the moon is made of blue cheese.

"I'm a possessive asshole. I don't want any guys thinking they have a chance with you when we're together."

"Duncan..."

"It's probably not fair to you. You've only had, well, me. And your college years should be about exploration. I'm hoping that because I'm older and wiser, you will believe what I'm saying when I tell you that it doesn't feel this right with just anyone."

She blinks like I'm speaking gibberish. "You witnessed me at my most awkward."

"I do remember the braces. The frizzy hair. Oh, and that time you stuffed your bra."

"I never!"

"Please. My friends were over playing Halo and you and Jules were going to the roller rink. You had…" I motion to her chest. "…pretty good-size grapefruits when you left. But the next morning, you were flatter than the pancakes we just ate."

She covers her face with her hands. "Oh my God. I didn't think you would notice."

"I thought it was cute." I uncover her face. "You're bigger than good-sized grapefruit now. I noticed that right away last night."

"Yeah, senior year I finally got boobs and they just kept growing and growing. I usually keep them under wraps. They get in my way a lot."

I put my hand on her chest and lean in for a kiss. "I'm glad they're here," I murmur against her lips. Pulling back, I look her in the eye. "There are no games here. No pretending. I have a thing for you and I want to see where it goes."

She nods. "What about Jules, though?"

Yeah. What about Jules?

Eleven

Ginger

I SNEAK INTO MY DORM room in case Jules is napping off her green beer hangover.

She's not.

Jules jumps off her bed. "I can't believe you got arrested last night!"

"I didn't. Not really. Luckily, your brother was just leaving the station and made sure I didn't get booked. I can't believe anyone would have thought I was a hooker, though. The one time I wear a dress..."

"Well, it was a very sexy dress," she laughs. "So then what happened? How did you end up at Duncan's house? When I talked to you guys, I thought he was taking you back here."

I walk gingerly over to my bed. My lady bits are very sore from losing their virginity to a man whose friends call him Horse. I plop down and wince. "I was pretty freaked out still, so Duncan didn't want to bring me back here if I was going to be alone. Then the weather got nasty and he lost power, so I just stayed there. I made him pancakes this morning to thank him." Okay, so that leaves off a giant, and I mean giant, portion of my evening. But baby steps. "How did your night go? How did you end up with a guy in Sussex dorm?"

"He and his friend were doing the same thing we were...escaping to a bar away from campus to avoid the usual douchery. His name is Gabe. I like him. Plus, he's good in bed." She pauses. "I'm sorry you lost out on your chance to punch your V-card last night. That dress was made for attracting suitable candidates.

"That dress was made for attracting vice police." I shake my head. Duncan and I decided I should be the one to tell Jules we hooked up, but now I wish I'd made him do it. "So, Jules..."

"Gabe has a cute roommate."

"Um..."

"We're going to a party tonight. The roommate will be there. I told Gabe I would bring you."

"So, here's the thing..."

She rolls onto her stomach and swings her legs back and forth. "Don't here's the thing me. Just because it didn't work out last night doesn't mean you can't save the weekend. It's one party. And it's not in a frat house."

"Jules, I'm sort of seeing someone and we agreed to not date anyone else while we see how things go."

She screws her face up. "Who did you meet last night? I thought you went to my brother's—" She sits up. "You fucked my brother?"

"Don't be mad."

"How...no...you can't have. I've heard the rumors about my brother. No way could you...not your first time. Did you guys cook this up to prank me?"

I move over to her bed and sit next to her. "It's not a prank."

"How did this happen?" She looks more shocked than mad. I hope that's a good sign.

"I don't know...the power was out and we were camped out in front of the fire talking and it just...happened. Are you mad?"

She thinks about it for a minute. "Not yet. Not at you anyway. But he shouldn't have—"

"I wanted to, Jules."

We're quiet for a minute. "But you're my friend."

"I'm your best friend. That hasn't changed."

"I thought you wanted to do it with a stranger. So you didn't have to see them again if it was awkward. You come home with me all the time on holidays and stuff. Will it be awkward to see your one night fling at my dad's birthday bowling party or Easter brunch?" She pauses. "Wait, you said you agreed not to see anyone else…"

I squeeze her hand. "He wants to date me. He wants to be my boyfriend."

She looks at me like "oh honey, no."

"I know what you're thinking. So I told him he had to be literal with me because relationships with humans confuse me. He told me in exact words. He wants to be exclusive and he wants me to call him boyfriend. Not fuck buddies."

Jules stands up. "I'm going to go for a walk. I need to be alone for a little while so I can process this."

"Okay. I'll be here when you're ready to talk."

I get a text from her a few minutes later. "It's fucking cold outside."

I laugh. "Sorry. Come back to the room. I'll go hang out in the lounge until you're ready."

"No. Stay."

She comes back in, kicks off her shoes, and gets under her covers. "I think it's going to rain again. And if it rains, it will probably be ice."

So now we're talking about the weather. "Yeah, probably."

She's quiet again. For about thirty seconds. "The rumors, though. About...Duncan's you know."

"True," I reply. They are very true.

"Rough first time."

"I took an Epsom salt bath for an hour before I came home."

"But he was nice to you?"

I smile. "He was so sweet. Yesterday, when you and I were getting ready to go out, I just wanted to get it over with, you know? But Duncan made it good for me. I swear."

"That's good. But you know...it's weird. You've always been mine. And I knew I'd have to share you someday because you're too awesome to never have a boyfriend. And I feel like a real bitch. But I don't like that I have to share you with my brother." I put my arm around her and hug her tightly. "I'm still yours. I love you and I always will. No one will ever replace you. I promise.

"We didn't plan it. Never in a million years would I have thought he would even be interested in me. He saw me almost get arrested for prostitution last night. Not an auspicious beginning. And oh my God, Jules, he remembers the night I stuffed my bra when we went skating."

Jules cracks up. "Shit. I forgot about that. He remembers?"

I start laughing then too. "I'm guessing he's seen most of my horribly embarrassing moments. I wish I could erase his memory like they do in *Men in Black*. I mean this is mortifying."

"You've seen his embarrassing moments, too."

"I don't remember him doing anything embarrassing."

Warm now, Jules kicks off the blankets. "I remember them all. I will dole them out to you one a day for the rest of your life if you want. Like an advent calendar."

We both start laughing, and it feels like the tension has been broken. We talk about Duncan for a while, and I feel like I can be honest with her about my feelings. I know she's a little bit jealous, but she accepts that I'm allowed to have a life outside of our friendship.

When she goes to her party, I stay in to nurse my poor abused vagina and study. Until I get a text from my new boyfriend.

"What are you wearing?"

Twelve

Duncan

I STARE AT MY PHONE like I'm fourteen years old waiting for a pretty girl to respond.

"Your shirt," she answers.

I like that she's still wearing my shirt.

I smile. "Good girl. Did it go okay with Jules?"

My phone buzzes and I realize she's calling me instead of answering my text. "Hey, baby."

"Hey," she says, her voice soft and sweet. "Jules and I talked and everything's good. We laughed about old times and I feel like we're in a good place."

"That's great to hear. I'm glad you guys are okay."

"I'm glad too. But now I'm all alone in my dorm room. What are you up to?"

"Laundry."

She laughs. "Laundry, huh? Sounds sexy."

I chuckle. "Oh yeah, nothing gets me going like separating my whites and colors."

She giggles. "Well, I could think of a few other things that might get you going."

My heart races at her words. "Like what?"

"I've been thinking a lot about the *Periodic Table of Elements*."

Fuck if I don't start to get a boner. "Before last night, that was the least sexy thing I could think of."

"That's what happens when your girlfriend is a nerd."

My girlfriend. Yesterday at this time, I didn't have a girlfriend. Despite everything moving so fast, it's not fast enough. I want her here. I want to know everything about her.

"I love that you're a nerd," I say, grinning foolishly to myself. "It's sexy as hell."

She giggles again, and I can imagine the way she bites her lip as she does. "Well, then get ready to be turned on. I have a surprise for you."

"Yeah? What?"

"I'm not wearing any panties."

I lick my lips, remembering how sweet she tasted. "Please tell me you've got the sexy glasses on though." I fucking love those big, dorky glasses.

"I do. Yes."

"And you're alone?"

"Yep."

I sit back in my chair. "If I was there, my tongue would be tracing circles around your nipples, making them hard and sensitive."

She lets out a soft moan over the phone. "Mmm, I wish you were here to do that."

"I wish I was there too, baby. But for now, I want you to touch yourself. Will you do that for me? Let me hear you come?"

"Yes," she breathes.

I close my eyes, imagining her in her bed, fingers slipping between her legs. "Tell me what you're doing, Ginger."

"I'm touching my breasts, teasing my nipples with my fingers," she whispers. "I'm starting to get wet already."

"Good girl," I murmur, my voice low. "I'm hard already too."

"Take it out, Duncan."

I reach down and unzip my jeans, slipping my hand inside to grip my hard length. "It's out," I whisper. It looks like a damn monster. How the hell did I fit that in her tiny pussy?

"Put your hand on it for me," she says softly.

I do as she asks, stroking myself slowly as I listen to her breathing become more and more labored.

"Are you touching your pussy?"

"Yes," she moans.

"I'm imagining it, Ginger. I'm imagining my fingers in you, how slick and wet you must be. It's driving me crazy." My breathing is becoming more ragged. I can't believe I'm having phone sex with my little sister's best friend.

"Duncan, I wish we were together right now. I can't make myself come the way you do it. I need you."

My heart thumps hard in my chest. She needs me. "You want words, baby? Do you want to hear my filthy words?"

"Yes," she whispers.

"Such a naughty girl." I close my eyes and squeeze the head of my dick so I don't come yet. "I'm imagining you beneath me, on your back, legs spread wide. Look at that pretty pussy. You're so wet."

She whimpers.

"I'm pushing my cock into you, inch by inch, until I'm buried deep."

"Oh God. Your cock is so big, Duncan."

"I know. But you can take it can't you?"

"Yes, I love it."

"You're all stretched out around me. I'm thrusting slowly, watching you bite your lip as you moan. I'm filling you up completely, and it feels so damn good. You're so tight and wet around me, Ginger. I can't get enough of you."

"Oh, Duncan..."

I grin. I can tell by her voice that she's close. "Nobody else can take this cock the way you can. You're such a dirty girl, and I love it. Everyone thinks you're so innocent, but we know the truth, don't we? We know how you really like it. How you need this big cock splitting you open."

"I'm going to come," she moans.

"Go ahead, baby. Come for me."

"You come too. Fill me up, Duncan. I need your cum inside me."

"Fuck." I can't stop myself. Not after that. I let out a deep groan as I come, imagining my cum spilling into her tight pussy.

She cries out my name as she comes on the other end of the line.

I'm a mess, cum all over my hand, my shirt, my pants.

We stay quiet for a few moments, until she finally speaks. "Wow. That was...unexpected."

I laugh. "Yeah, it was. You're amazing, Ginger."

We make plans to go on a coffee date Wednesday and a real date Friday. The case I'm working on cancels our Wednesday plans, and by Friday I need to see her so fucking much I nearly bite everyone's head off at work.

I pick her up from the dorm. She's too quiet when I open the truck door for her. She packed an overnight bag, but she looks the opposite of excited.

"You don't have to stay tonight. If you don't want to," I say, pulling out of the dorm parking lot.

"Do you not want me to?"

"Of course I want you to. What's going on? We just spoke last night and you were fine. Are you having second thoughts?"

She shakes her head. "I'm just nervous. I knew I would ruin this."

"Nothing is ruined. You just need to tell me what is going on."

"I'm worried that...well, you didn't notice me until the dress. And I'm not," she looks down at her simple outfit, "dressed like that. And maybe I'm not sexy enough now. When I'm being the real me."

"Yes, I noticed you in the dress. It was like waving a red cape in front of a bull. But that dress isn't why I'm attracted to you."

She's wringing her hands together tightly. "I'm sorry. You might have to deal with my insecurity issues for a little while."

"I don't mind." I take her hand in mine and pull it up to my lips, kissing her knuckles softly. She looks up at me, and suddenly I'm lost in her eyes. "You keep looking at me like that and I will forget that I promised to feed you."

"I'm actually starving. But I promise to look at you like this after dinner."

There's my girl. We pull up to the restaurant and go inside to have our first date. Ginger may only be twenty, but she's wise. And fucking hilarious once she relaxes. I know it's fast, but I feel like I just always want to be with her.

When we get to my house, I can see the nerves creeping up on Ginger again. She's fidgeting with the hem of her shirt and avoiding my gaze. I know what she needs. I need it too. I pull her into my arms and kiss her deeply. She melts against me, her body molding to mine. I can feel her hands gripping my shirt tightly, pulling me closer. I break away from the kiss, trailing my lips down her neck, nibbling on the skin. She moans softly, arching her neck to give me more access.

I feel her hands move down to my belt, unfastening it quickly. I pull away from her, "We don't have to. If you want to wait."

"I want to. Very much."

I lead her to my bedroom, suddenly fighting my own nerves. Maybe it was a fluke that she was able to take all of my cock the first time. Maybe it will hurt her this time. She's so petite, and I'm like a fucking beast.

"Would it be okay if..."

"Anything," I reply when she doesn't finish her thought.

"Could I just...I want to explore...um...you. Your body. With my hands and my mouth. If that's okay."

I feel myself grow harder as she shyly admits her desires. "Yes, of course. Anything you want.

Thirteen

Ginger

DUNCAN REMOVES ALL his clothing and reclines on his bed. I strip down to my bra and panties and climb on the bed. His cock is, well, disturbingly large, so I start at the top of his body instead.

I kiss and lick my way along his jawline, down his neck, and across his chest. His muscles ripple, tensing and relaxing under my lips.

Inhaling deeply, I take in his masculine scent and feel my own heart racing. I don't even know how to describe it. A hint of spice, a hint of leather, and something else, something that I can't quite put my finger on. "You smell amazing, Duncan," I murmur against his skin as I trail my tongue down his chest. He groans in response as I continue to explore the planes of his chest, my hands running along his abs and my tongue dipping into his navel.

"Fuck. Baby, you're driving me crazy."

I chuckle against his skin and continue to explore.

He's so sturdy. Solid. He's got muscles for sure, but he's also got a bit of a dad bod, thick and solid. I stroke his furry chest and swirl my hands through the patch of hair on his stomach. I'm so glad he's not like the guys who wax everything away, leaving their skin glistening and smooth. I love his scruffy, masculine look. I didn't know I had a preference. But I really do.

I slide down to his tree trunk legs, running my hands up and down them, over and over. He's so powerful. So masculine. He appeals to the part of me that knows he'd protect our cave from a saber-tooth tiger, but also, he'd pull my hair and fuck me against its stone walls.

He gasps when I lick a trail up his inner thigh. I take my time, teasing the sensitive skin there, making sure to leave him panting and desperate for more.

He grabs my hair and pulls me until I find myself at the base of his cock. "Need you," he says.

"Don't rush me. I'm exploring," I tease.

He growls, pushing his hips up and into my face. "Please. I'm dying."

He's so big. Big is too small a word. He smells good here, too, though. A clean musk that sends my stomach to flutter. I nuzzle the base and the skin covering his balls, pressing a kiss there.

"Fuck, baby," he moans.

His testicles are huge, which I guess I didn't notice last time, but of course they are, considering his extra large cock. The sac heavy and full and the thought of all that cum inside his balls makes me tingle with anticipation. I flick my tongue over them before taking one into my mouth, swirling it around. He hisses and his hips move against my face.

I pull back, sort of enjoying the torture I'm dishing out.

His cock looks like a weapon by this point. So hard and ready. The shaft is a dusky pink, but the head is a darker, richer shade. It's intimidating, but I want it. I want it bad.

I lick the wet tip and Duncan gasps.

"Mmmm. You taste good, Duncan."

His breathing hitches, and he grips the sheets beneath him.

I want to rub my body all over him. I get an idea and unclasp my bra. Moving his legs apart, I kneel between them and lower, fitting his giant cock between my breasts.

"Fuck. Ginger, you're going to make me come."

I squeeze my tits around the base of his shaft and slowly move up and down. I need more slick, so I use the liberal amounts of precum he's leaking to lubricate his cock. The sensation of his hard shaft between my soft mounds is so naughty, and I can feel my own desire pooling in my core.

This time when I reach the tip, I stretch my mouth wide around the glistening head of his cock and suck before releasing him and moving back down.

"Killing me, baby."

The slow tease is killing me too. He sits up and with a burst of masculine energy, flips me around so I'm facing his feet. He lays back down and yanks me over his face, diving into me with a hunger that leaves me feeling completely undone. His hands grasp my hips, probably bruising my skin, while his mouth devours my pussy.

Duncan isn't acting like Mr. Nice Guy anymore. He's feral without an ounce of gentleness. The noises he makes when he sucks and licks and bites are more animal, more beast, than human. He's growling into my pussy, a deep and guttural sound that vibrates straight through to my toes.

I open my eyes, and there it is, his juicy cock pointing right at my face. I open my mouth and slide him in. Judging from how much of his shaft is still in my grip, I'm not taking very much into my mouth. But my mouth is nonetheless full, and his precum coats my tongue.

It's so hard to pay attention to his cock when he's licking and sucking me like his life depends on it. But I do my best to move my head in time with his thrusts, taking him all the way to the back once, causing me to gag and cough.

He pulls me off his dick.

"Wait, I want it, Duncan."

He lifts my body off his face an inch so he can talk. "Just the head, tonight. Just suck on the head. We'll try going deeper another night, sweetheart."

And then he's back in my pussy, making me incoherent. I swirl my tongue around the head of his cock, using my hands to stroke. We fall into a rhythm, his tongue working my clit and my hands working his shaft while I suck. He's panting and I'm moaning. I can feel him tensing and I know he's about to come. He pauses his feast of me. "If you don't want a mouthful, switch to just your hands."

I definitely want a mouthful!

I take the head of his cock into my mouth as far as I can.

"Baby—"

"Mmmm," I moan, knowing the vibrations will feel good. (Thanks, *Cosmopolitan Magazine*.)

"Fuck," he groans as he pulses hot cum into my mouth. It's warm and salty. I feel so wicked and naughty and sexy and all the things I never thought I could be.

The taste of him unlocks another level of primal lust in me. I swallow most of it, licking my lips to try and catch what spills out.

"Fuck. My little sex goddess," he says. "That was so good. You drank my cum like such a good girl."

The praise knocks my heart around in my ribcage.

"I loved it, Duncan. I want to do it again and again. You taste so good."

"Get that pussy back on my face," he says and attacks my clit.

My entire body shakes as I come, but he doesn't let me up when I try to move away, instead just keeps moving my pussy all over his face. I'm over-sensitized, but he doesn't let me up.

"Duncan, I—"

"I can't get enough," he says, inserting two fingers into me and pumping them in and out. I tense around him when he finds a spot that sends sparks through my body.

"It's too much." Whatever he's doing is too much. My skin feels like it's cracking to let the building pressure of another orgasm out of my body. I think I have to pee. "Please," I beg.

"You're going to fucking come again," he growls, pushing his fingers deeper and using his tongue to rub my clit. I cry out as a geyser of fluid erupts from me, pleasure and relief washing over me in waves.

My body buckles as my soul just...leaves my body. What just happened? Did I just...?

"You squirted. God, you're the best. Nobody has ever done that for me before."

"Squirted?" I roll off him, but he pulls me around into his arms. I'm not sure if I should be embarrassed or proud.

"It's an orgasm, only more intense and wetter. Female ejaculation. You are so amazing."

"So, it's not gross?"

"No, it's beautiful. You're incredible."

"But it's messy."

"Babe, cum is messy. That's part of the fun. Cleaning up can be fun too. We can take a shower together."

"We could if you hadn't rendered all my limbs useless. I don't think I can move a muscle right now."

"Perfect. Now you're completely at my mercy." He grins devilishly and I can't help but laugh.

He helps me up and we head to the shower. After everything that just transpired, you'd think I would have no modesty left, but the bright lights of the bathroom make me feel so exposed.

Duncan notices and wraps his arms around me. "You don't need to feel shy. Your body is amazing. It's everything. Honest."

The warm water cascades over us, washing away any traces of our previous activities.

I sigh. "It's just that...I'm not...grr. I just feel like my body is just meh."

He takes the shower gel and pours some into his hands. "Your body turns me on more than I've ever been in my life. If anything, I should be the one who's self-conscious here."

"You?" I scoff, as he begins to wash my body. "Your body is like an A+ in primal perfection."

"I could work out more. I'm a husky boy."

I take the gel bottle and get to work on him. "I love your body, Duncan. It's strong and powerful and it turns me on so much."

He leans down and kisses me. "You make me want to say things to you that it's way too soon to say."

"Duncan..."

"I don't want to push you into something you aren't ready for. You're barely into your twenties and shouldn't rush into anything with me. Or anyone. But you should know I plan on staying the course with you. I know your worth and I'm not going to screw this up."

I put my hand over his heart. "I've been in love with you for ten years. I don't think it's possible to rush me at this point. You're the one who just now noticed me."

He chuckles. "Slow learner. I apologize." He takes my face into his hands and kisses me.

We finish washing up in a comfortable silence and after we dry off, he carries me to the bed and tucks me in. Then gets in and spoons behind me.

"How are you feeling?"

"Better than ever. But we didn't..."

"We will. I promise. Tomorrow. I just want to hold you tonight. You making me pancakes tomorrow?"

"You'll have to pay me in orgasms in the morning first."

"Deal."

Fourteen

——

Duncan

TWO MONTHS LATER

"I don't think this is the appropriate venue to break the news," Ginger says, refusing to get out of the truck.

"Oh my God, GinGin," my sister complains from the backseat. "My parents are going to be happy. What are you worried about?"

We're at the bowling alley for my Dad's birthday party. Ginger usually comes with Jules anyway, so they are expecting her. But today we're going to tell them we are a couple.

"What if they aren't happy though?"

"Baby, our parents love you. If they are mad at anyone, it will be me for taking advantage of my little sister's best friend. I'm the villain here."

Jules agrees.

Ginger scoffs and pushes her glasses up. "You're not the villain. We're both adults. You're not even that much older than I am. I mean, if you dated me when I started my crush on you it would have been weird since you were sixteen and I was ten. But twenty-six and twenty is no big deal."

"Exactly," Jules replies. "Can you at least let me out of the truck you guys?"

We get out of the truck and let my sister out of the backseat. Inside, the far two lanes are decorated for Pop's annual birthday celebration. Ginger walks about five paces ahead of me, her arms wrapped around her middle. I have to catch up to her and snake my arm around her. "We're doing this."

"I don't want to ruin his birthday."

I stop us and Jules goes ahead. "It's not going to ruin his birthday to find out his only son is finally in love."

Her eyes get huge under those glasses. "You love me?"

Well, that wasn't how I intended to say it to her the first time, but this will have to make do. "I love you more than anything. I've never felt like this before."

I kiss her softly and her arms go around my neck. The whistles from the far lane make us both jump back.

Ginger gives me a shaky smile and waves to everyone. Jules is standing next to my parents, who look shell-shocked.

I take Ginger's hand and we finish the long, green mile to the party. My cousin claps me on the back hard, and my partner from work, Dan, offers me a beer. He knows how nervous Ginger and I have been about this day. I wave him away and we stop in front of my folks.

"Happy birthday, Pops," I say.

"What's going on here?" my mom asks.

"Ginger and I have been dating for a couple of months," I tell them. "We kept it to ourselves until I knew she wasn't going to throw me over."

Ginger hits my arm. "Shut up."

My mom looks worried. "She's a nice girl, Duncan. Your sister's best friend."

"I know she's a nice girl, Mom. That's one of the reasons why I love her."

My mom gets tears in her eyes and her whole demeanor changes. "My baby!" She hugs me and then hugs Ginger. "You've been like a daughter to me since you were a little girl, Ginger. I'm surprised, but very happy. So long as Duncan treats you right."

"Mom!" I say. "I'm your actual son. Shouldn't you be more worried about me?"

That's when my dad grabs my arm and indicates the bar. "A word, son."

Ginger looks worried, but I kiss her cheek and go with my dad to the bar. He doesn't say anything until after we get our beers. "She's young."

"Yeah, Dad. I know."

He looks a little older than he did a few minutes ago. "We raised you right, I know you don't play with women's feelings. But Ginger, she's special. She's very special to us all. I worry."

My dad is the best man I know. "I love her. I'd marry her tomorrow if...well, like you said, she's young. But I'm not playing with her feelings. She's got all the power here. She's the one, Dad."

My dad laughs into the neck of his beer. "She used to watch you. With that headgear on her face and those great big black glasses. She had hearts in her eyes. I never thought you'd look back at her the same way." He takes a deep breath and claps me on the back. "Be good to her. She deserves it."

"I will, Dad," I say, taking a swig of my beer. "I will."

We rejoin the party in time to see Ginger roll another gutter ball down the lane. In all the years we've come here for my dad's birthday, I don't think she's ever hit an actual pin.

After the cake and the end of the party, we drop my sister off at the dorms and I take Ginger home. We're relaxing on the couch and she looks less pinched than she did earlier.

"I told you it would be fine."

"Your mom told me she's been saving some embarrassing pictures of you for the day when you brought a serious girl home. I get to see them next time I go over there."

"Hey! That's not fair." I flip us so she's under me. "You know what else isn't fair? I told you I loved you today." I say, grinding into her.

"Yeah you did." She's not saying it back, but her eyes are sparkling with mischief.

I grab her wrists and pin them above her head. "And?"

"And?"

"And what, babe?" I say, lowering my lips to hers. She giggles, trying to wriggle out of my grasp, but I hold her tight.

"And I love you too," she whispers against my mouth, and I feel a surge of warmth in my chest. I kiss her deeply, pouring all my love into it, and I can tell she feels it too.

"I'm so glad I get to love you, Ginger," I say, my words muffled in her hair.

"Me too."

I kiss her lips and then say against her mouth, "The best night of my life was when you got busted for hooking."

I've still got her pinned beneath me, so she can't claw me like she wants to. She bites my bottom lip. "You will regret that."

I will regret nothing.

Epilogue

Ginger

FIVE YEARS LATER, ST. Patrick's Day

I come out of the bathroom into our honeymoon suite and find my husband pouring champagne. His tux tie hangs around his neck, the sleeves of his white shirt are rolled up around his thick forearms.

Duncan whistles through his teeth, taking me in.

"You look so fucking hot."

I smile and cross the room to take a glass of the champagne. The green silk negligee swishes softly against my skin, it's cut very similar to the dress that I wore the night we got together. I was hoping it was just the right amount of slutty, and I think I can say it very much is.

I take a sip, then run my hand down his chest. "Wanna date, mister?"

"How much, baby?"

Since I have no idea what a hooker might charge, I shrug. "Everything you have to give, mister."

"Deal."

"Your heart."

"Done."

"Your soul."

"Already yours."

"Your truck?"

"Don't push it."

Duncan takes my glass and sets it on the table with his. Then my world turns upside down as he throws me over his shoulder and carries me to the bed.

He tosses me down and makes quick work of the rest of his wedding clothes. I watch in awe, just as infatuated with his body as I always have been.

The cock doesn't scare me anymore. Though, the stretch still stings a little every time. He's got it in his big hand now, pointing it at me. He gives it a long slow stroke and moisture pools between my legs just like always.

"Bring that here," I tell him. "Let me show you how much I love you."

He stands at the edge of the bed and I swirl my tongue around the head. He takes a step back. "Not tonight. You get me all worked up, and I'll come down your throat."

"You say that like it's a bad thing."

"You told me I couldn't come for three days so I had the best chance of putting a baby in you tonight. I'm not coming in your throat."

I have to smile at his eagerness to get me pregnant. He takes this moment to push me onto my back and pull my ass to the edge of the bed. He kneels there and pushes my nightie up over my hips, spreading me in front of him. "You get to come as many times as possible, though."

And then his mouth is on me.

Duncan enjoys eating my pussy more than anyone should enjoy anything. It's obscene, the sounds he makes, the moans he lets out as he laps at me. The pleasure builds and builds until I'm shaking and panting and begging for more.

He adds two fingers, fucking me with them until I come so hard that I'm hoarse. And then he doesn't stop. My instinct is always to move away from the stimulation at this point, but Duncan knows my body well. And he knows what he wants from it.

"It's too much," I moan.

"It's not. I'm not stopping until you squirt, Mrs. O'Malley." He reaches for that spot inside me that makes stars dance in front of my eyes. Every nerve in my body is snapping, my pleasure is a painful ecstasy that I can't escape. His tongue works my clit and I can't breathe.

And then it happens, I'm quaking and screaming, my wetness flooding his hand and spilling over his knuckles.

He draws away and wipes his chin, grinning at me. "That, that right there is why I love you."

My heart is pounding and my skin is so sensitive that his touch sends me into a new wave of pleasure. I'm helpless in his arms, unable to do anything but bask in the afterglow of my orgasm.

"I love you too," I whisper.

He kisses me, and I reach up to grab the back of his neck, making him moan into my mouth. His hips press into mine and I can feel the heat of his desire against my thigh.

"I've got something else for you."

"I hope so."

His huge cock is dripping in precum. He moves very slowly, pushing into me inch by inch. There's so much natural lubrication between the two of us, but the stretch around that flared head still makes me gasp.

He pauses, waiting for me to adjust, and then begins to move. His thrusts are slow and deliberate, each one sending a jolt of pleasure through my body. His hands are everywhere, squeezing my hips, pinching my nipples, stroking my hair.

I'm shaking, trying to keep up with him, but it's no use. He's in control and I'm just along for the ride. I'm teetering on the edge of orgasm when he reaches down and circles my clit with his thumb. I'm done for.

I scream out his name as I come, my body shuddering around him.

"You're such a good girl. Such a good fucking girl. I'm going to fill you with cum," he growls.

He slams into me, his dick throbbing inside me. He comes with a guttural roar, his hot seed spilling inside me. His release seems to go on and on, just when I think he's done, he pulses more cum into me. His arms wrap around me, holding me tight as he kisses my neck. We lay there, panting and sweaty, our skin sticking together.

"Jesus," he says finally. "Did we die? I was in a tunnel. There was a light..." He lays his head on my heart. "Who knew banging a married chick was going to be so hot."

I giggle. "We need a shower."

"In a minute."

After we clean up, we have a much-needed snack from room service and curl into bed again.

"Are you sure you don't regret not going someplace exotic for our honeymoon? We could probably still get away for a few days someplace nice."

I shake my head. "No way. That puppy is coming home with us tomorrow."

Instead of taking our vacation time someplace warm and sunny, we opted to spend one night in the honeymoon suite near home so we could pick up our puppy from the shelter and spend two weeks getting to know our little guy.

And make a concerted effort to impregnate me.

After five years, I can honestly say that getting arrested for prostitution was the best thing that ever happened to me.

And green is my lucky color.

Did you love *Just My Luck*? Then you should read *All Together*[1] by Brill Harper!

[2]

Nerdy Penelope has never even been kissed. But that was before her hot college roommates offer to be her study buddies...in the bedroom.

It's basically chiseled bodies, piercing eyes, strong hands, and testosterone twenty-four-seven at her house. Now she's got two virile men giving her a very adult education, and the one thing she's always been good at is being a star pupil. The best part is she doesn't have to choose—she gets them both and can literally do anything she wants to them.

Except keep them.

Author Confession: You know and I know that I will only ever deliver you an HEA, so sit back and enjoy the sweet, filthy love story

---

1. https://books2read.com/u/bppVYX

2. https://books2read.com/u/bppVYX

of a nerdy heroine and two hunky alphamallows. Let me know which one steals your heart more. I bet you can't choose either.

About the Author

Unfailingly filthy...and super sweet

Brill's books are filthy/sweet for when you're in the mood for something a little over the top. Okay, a lot over the top. Sorry, not sorry.

Brill Harper is represented by Deidre Knight of The Knight Agency.

www.ingramcontent.com/pod-product-compliance
Lightning Source LLC
Chambersburg PA
CBHW031441130726
47989CB00003B/1236